1 6 FEB 2017

1 2 NOV 2018

2 6 NOV 2019

17·12·21

Southwark Council

Canada Water Library
21 Surrey Quays Road
London
SE16 7AR
020 7525 2000

Please return/renew this item by
the last date shown.
Books may also be renewed by
phone and Internet.

D0184924

First published 1993
by Walker Books Ltd
87 Vauxhall Walk
London SE11 5HJ

This edition published 1995

28 30 29

Illustrations © 1993 Julie Lacome

The right of Julie Lacome to be identified as author
of this work has been asserted by her in accordance with the
Copyright, Designs and Patents Act 1988

This book has been typeset in Bembo

Printed in China

All rights reserved

British Library Cataloguing in Publication Data:
a catalogue record for this book
is available from the British Library

ISBN 978-0-7445-3643-0

www.walker.co.uk

Walking Through The Jungle

illustrated by

Julie Lacome

WALKER BOOKS

AND SUBSIDIARIES

LONDON • BOSTON • SYDNEY • AUCKLAND

Walking through the jungle,
What do you see?
Can you hear a noise?
What could it be?

SSSsss

Over there!
A snake
looking
for his tea.

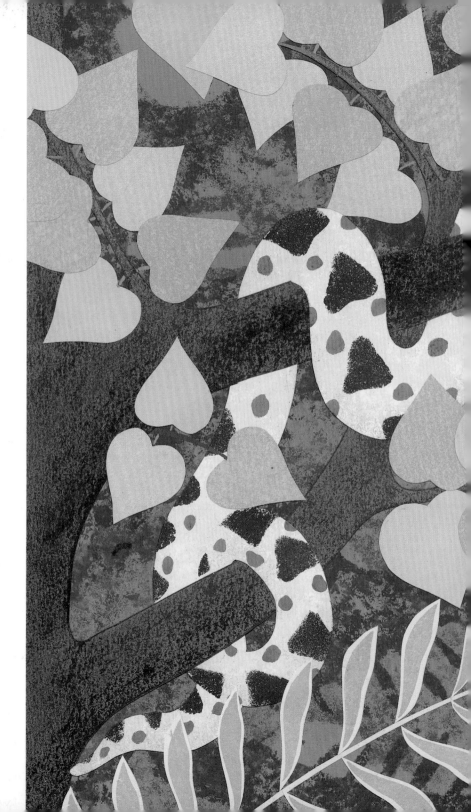

Creeping through the jungle,
What do you see?
Can you hear a noise?
What could it be?

grrrrrr

Over there!
A tiger
looking
for his tea.

Running through the jungle,
What do you see?
Can you hear a noise?
What could it be?

trump trump

Over there!
An elephant
looking
for his tea.

Leaping through the jungle,
What do you see?
Can you hear a noise?
What could it be?

roarrrr

Over there!
A lion
looking
for his tea.

Swinging through the jungle,
What do you see?
Can you hear a noise?
What could it be?

chitter chatter

Over there!
A monkey
looking
for his tea.

Wading through the jungle,
What do you see?
Can you hear a noise?
What could it be?

snap snap

snap snap

Over there!
A crocodile
looking
for his tea…

Hope it isn't me!

WALKER BOOKS is the world's leading independent publisher of children's books. Working with the best authors and illustrators we create books for all ages, from babies to teenagers – books your child will grow up with and always remember. So…

FOR THE BEST CHILDREN'S BOOKS, LOOK FOR THE BEAR